My Music Journal

Year: _____

Name: _____

Address: _____

_____

Phone: _____

Teacher: _____

Phone: _____

Table of Contents

Lesson Assignments .... 4 - 27

Journal Entries .... 28 - 33

Music History Time-line .... 34 - 39

Staff Paper .... 40 - 47

Keyboard Guide .... front cover

Dictionary of Terms .... back cover

HAL•LEONARD® CORPORATION

7777 W. BLUEMOUND RD. P.O. BOX 13819 MILWAUKEE, WI 53213

Visit Hal Leonard Online at
www.halleonard.com

A Letter To Students

Ways You Can Use Your Music Journal

This journal will help you organize and enjoy your practice time – the hours you spend taking charge of your own learning and making music on your own.

1.   Make music every day.

With your teacher or a parent, fill in your weekly schedule. Remember to include your outside activities such as sports practice, other lessons, and school and family events.

Consider your whole schedule and choose the time you will practice. Although you will want to work on your technique and new pieces every day, the balance of practice activities can shift according to your weekly schedule.

Even if you have a day that seems to give you no time to practice, **take time to play!** Choose your favorite piece and enjoy it. Ask your friends and family to listen. Often we forget to practice a piece at the most important time of all – after we already know it!

2.   Read your assignments.

Your lesson assignment is a guide for your week's work. Read it carefully and follow the instructions. Remember that your teacher has spent years learning to play and knows exactly how it feels to struggle with new music. Your teacher's practice suggestions will make your learning easier and help you bring the music to life!

3.   Keep a record of your musical experiences.

When you learn to play an instrument, you join the world of musicians. Become aware of the music you hear around you and learn more about the artists who create it. Keep a record of concerts you have attended and the recorded performances and music books you especially enjoy.

Record your own musical journey by filling in the list of your favorite pieces and your own performances. Include pictures of yourself and your teacher, parents, and friends.

4.   Keep your music journals from year to year.

As you leaf through your music journals in the years to come, you will watch your skills develop, your musical interests blossom, and your list of favorite music grow. We wish you success and joy in your own special musical journey.

A Letter To Parents

Ways You Can Help Demonstrate The Importance Of Music

1. **Encourage your child to play for others.**

   Every few weeks, make it a point to ask your child to perform for the family. Talk to teachers at school about opportunities for your child to play a piece or two for class. Find out if your church will allow your child to perform before or during a church service.

   If you play the piano or another instrument, offer to play duets with your child.
   If you don't play, ask your child to teach you one of his/her pieces, or the right-hand melody to one of your favorite songs.

2. **Go to concerts together.**

   Take your child to concerts of any kind - perhaps the band or orchestra concert at the local high school, a symphony, jazz, or church concert; or a summer music festival show.

3. **Visit an art museum.**

   Visit an art museum and introduce your child to the work of artists who were contemporaries of the music composers of the same period.

4. **Develop a home musical library.**

   Give your child a CD or cassette gift of *Peter And The Wolf* (by Prokofiev), *Carnival Of The Animals* (by Saint-Saens), or *A Young Person's Guide To The Orchestra* (by Benjamin Britten). All three have charming narratives interwoven with the music.

5. **Go to the library.**

   Borrow CDs or cassettes from your local library - not only classical music, but jazz, blues, gospel, musical theater, opera, etc.

   Encourage your child to read about the lives of famous performers or composers. Watch for special performances on public television, or rent a music video, such as the pianist Vladimer Horowitz playing his Moscow concerts.

6. **Visit your local print music store often.**

   Your child will enjoy learning learn new music he has selected himself. Never allow photocopying of print music; explain that composers receive their income through royalties.

Lesson Assignments

Date: **Feb. 3**

① p. 24 + 25   Ode to Joy   Play in C Finger Position
"Legato"   Transpose to G Finger Position
smooth + connected   Try different key signatures!

② Elementary Scalebook : Go as far as you would like

p. 26 + 27 Practice musical patterns + sequences
p. 32, 33, 34, 35, 36 (and transpose), 38 + 39 — use dynamics
                          ᐳ = accent (stronger than other notes)

Weekly Schedule p. 40, 41, 42, 43, 44, 45, 46 + 47

Sunday	Monday	Tuesday	Wednesday	Thursday	Friday	Saturday
Practice Record:						

Date: **Feb. 17**

① p. 51 Camptown Races — duet

② p. 52 + 53 Eine Kleine Nachtmusik

③ p. 54   New World Symphony

④ p. 57 Jingle Bells

⑤ Scales + Chords — play duets next week

Weekly Schedule

Sunday	Monday	Tuesday	Wednesday	Thursday	Friday	Saturday
Practice Record:						

Lesson Assignments

Date: <u>Feb. 24</u>

① Scales + Chords p. 20 + 21   Songs + Transposing

② Scales + Chords   starts p. 22   As many as you are comfortable

③ p. 58-59 Royal Procession

④ p. 60 + 61   Broken Chords + 3rd

⑤ p. 62 - 63   Bass Clef Melodies

Weekly Schedule ⑥ p. 64 + 65

Sunday	Monday	Tuesday	Wednesday	Thursday	Friday	Saturday
Practice Record:						

Date: <u>March 3</u>

<u>Scales and Chords Book</u>
p. 20 + 21 Try transposing to a different key!
Continue on minor scales - Five Finger.

<u>Lesson Book</u>
p. 68, 69, 70, 71, 72 + 73 + 74 + 75

Theory Time if you have time!

Weekly Schedule

Sunday	Monday	Tuesday	Wednesday	Thursday	Friday	Saturday
Practice Record:						

Lesson Assignments

Date: <u>March 10</u>

<u>Scales and Chords</u>

p. 20 + 21   Transposing   p. 34-35 Practice songs but no
p. 30 + 31   Minor Arpeggios   transposing

p. 72   Transpose   m 9-16
p. 75   Happy Birthday
p. 76   English Folk Song
p. 77   Gavotte
p. 79   Simple Gifts

Weekly Schedule

Sunday	Monday	Tuesday	Wednesday	Thursday	Friday	Saturday
Practice Record:						

Date: <u>April 7</u>

p. 20 + 21   Songs for Transposing

p. 34 + 35   Jazzy Dance etc. Transposing

p. 36 - 39   Cadences

p. 80 - 81   Rhythm Drills and info
p. 82 - 83   Moon on the River
p. 84 - 85   500 Year Old Melody
p. 86 - 87   Reveille

Weekly Schedule

Sunday	Monday	Tuesday	Wednesday	Thursday	Friday	Saturday

Lesson Assignments

Date: April

* Be sure we do ear-training next time!

Scales and Chords
- p. 20 + 21 Continue transposing to many different keys.
- p. 34 + 35 Jazzy Dance, Little March + Dance — transposing.
- p. 36 - 39 Cadences
- p. 80 + 81 Rhythm
- p. 82 + 83 Moon on the Water — duet!
- p. 84 + 85 500 Year Old Melody — duet!
- p. 86 + 87 Reveille — duet! — Transpose
- p. 88 + 89 Arpeggios
- p. 90 + 91 When the Saints Go Marching In

Weekly Schedule p. 92 - 93 African Celebration

Interval: The distance between notes.

2nd is line to a space or space to a line "step"

3rd is line to line or space to space "skip"

Sunday	Monday	Tuesday	Wednesday	Thursday	Friday	Saturday
Practice Record:						

Date: May

* Practice counting outloud. Count without playing sometime.

p. 104 Chromatic scale; going up and down by half steps.

p. 105 Half-Time Band

p. 106 - 107 Greensleeves

Flat: Lowers a note ½ step

p. 108 - 109 Flats,
p. 110 - 111 Sleeping Beauty Waltz
p. 112 - 113 Summer Mountain Rain
p. 114 - 115 Major Pentascales

Weekly Schedule p. 116 - 119

Sharp: Raises a note ½ step.
Interval: Distance between notes.

Sunday	Monday	Tuesday	Wednesday	Thursday	Friday	Saturday
Practice Record:						

Lesson Assignments

Date: _____

Weekly Schedule

Sunday	Monday	Tuesday	Wednesday	Thursday	Friday	Saturday
Practice Record:						

Date: _____

Weekly Schedule

Sunday	Monday	Tuesday	Wednesday	Thursday	Friday	Saturday
Practice Record:						

Lesson Assignments

Date: _____

Weekly Schedule

Sunday	Monday	Tuesday	Wednesday	Thursday	Friday	Saturday
Practice Record:						

Date: _____

Weekly Schedule

Sunday	Monday	Tuesday	Wednesday	Thursday	Friday	Saturday
Practice Record:						

Lesson Assignments

Date: _____

Weekly Schedule

Sunday	Monday	Tuesday	Wednesday	Thursday	Friday	Saturday
Practice Record:						

Date: _____

Weekly Schedule

Sunday	Monday	Tuesday	Wednesday	Thursday	Friday	Saturday
Practice Record:						

Lesson Assignments

Date: _____

Weekly Schedule

Sunday	Monday	Tuesday	Wednesday	Thursday	Friday	Saturday
Practice Record:						

Date: _____

Weekly Schedule

Sunday	Monday	Tuesday	Wednesday	Thursday	Friday	Saturday
Practice Record:						

Lesson Assignments

Date: _____

Weekly Schedule

Sunday	Monday	Tuesday	Wednesday	Thursday	Friday	Saturday
Practice Record:						

Date: _____

Weekly Schedule

Sunday	Monday	Tuesday	Wednesday	Thursday	Friday	Saturday
Practice Record:						

Lesson Assignments

Date: _____

Weekly Schedule

Sunday	Monday	Tuesday	Wednesday	Thursday	Friday	Saturday
Practice Record:						

Date: _____

Weekly Schedule

Sunday	Monday	Tuesday	Wednesday	Thursday	Friday	Saturday
Practice Record:						

Lesson Assignments

Date: _____

Weekly Schedule

Sunday	Monday	Tuesday	Wednesday	Thursday	Friday	Saturday
Practice Record:						

Date: _____

Weekly Schedule

Sunday	Monday	Tuesday	Wednesday	Thursday	Friday	Saturday
Practice Record:						

Lesson Assignments

Date: _____

Weekly Schedule

Sunday	Monday	Tuesday	Wednesday	Thursday	Friday	Saturday
Practice Record:						

Date: _____

Weekly Schedule

Sunday	Monday	Tuesday	Wednesday	Thursday	Friday	Saturday
Practice Record:						

Lesson Assignments

Date: _____

Weekly Schedule

Sunday	Monday	Tuesday	Wednesday	Thursday	Friday	Saturday
Practice Record:						

Date: _____

Weekly Schedule

Sunday	Monday	Tuesday	Wednesday	Thursday	Friday	Saturday
Practice Record:						

Lesson Assignments

Date: _____

Weekly Schedule

Sunday	Monday	Tuesday	Wednesday	Thursday	Friday	Saturday
Practice Record:						

Date: _____

Weekly Schedule

Sunday	Monday	Tuesday	Wednesday	Thursday	Friday	Saturday
Practice Record:						

Lesson Assignments

Date: _____

Weekly Schedule

Sunday	Monday	Tuesday	Wednesday	Thursday	Friday	Saturday
Practice Record:						

Date: _____

Weekly Schedule

Sunday	Monday	Tuesday	Wednesday	Thursday	Friday	Saturday
Practice Record:						

Lesson Assignments

Date: _____

Weekly Schedule

Sunday	Monday	Tuesday	Wednesday	Thursday	Friday	Saturday
Practice Record:						

Date: _____

Weekly Schedule

Sunday	Monday	Tuesday	Wednesday	Thursday	Friday	Saturday
Practice Record:						

Lesson Assignments

Date: _____

Weekly Schedule

Sunday	Monday	Tuesday	Wednesday	Thursday	Friday	Saturday
Practice Record:						

Date: _____

Weekly Schedule

Sunday	Monday	Tuesday	Wednesday	Thursday	Friday	Saturday
Practice Record:						

Lesson Assignments

Date: _____

Weekly Schedule

Sunday	Monday	Tuesday	Wednesday	Thursday	Friday	Saturday
Practice Record:						

Date: _____

Weekly Schedule

Sunday	Monday	Tuesday	Wednesday	Thursday	Friday	Saturday
Practice Record:						

Lesson Assignments

Date: _____

Weekly Schedule

Sunday	Monday	Tuesday	Wednesday	Thursday	Friday	Saturday
Practice Record:						

Date: _____

Weekly Schedule

Sunday	Monday	Tuesday	Wednesday	Thursday	Friday	Saturday
Practice Record:						

Lesson Assignments

Date: _____

Weekly Schedule

Sunday	Monday	Tuesday	Wednesday	Thursday	Friday	Saturday
Practice Record:						

Date: _____

Weekly Schedule

Sunday	Monday	Tuesday	Wednesday	Thursday	Friday	Saturday
Practice Record:						

Lesson Assignments

Date: _____

Weekly Schedule

Sunday	Monday	Tuesday	Wednesday	Thursday	Friday	Saturday
Practice Record:						

Date: _____

Weekly Schedule

Sunday	Monday	Tuesday	Wednesday	Thursday	Friday	Saturday
Practice Record:						

Lesson Assignments

Date: _____

Weekly Schedule

Sunday	Monday	Tuesday	Wednesday	Thursday	Friday	Saturday
Practice Record:						

Date: _____

Weekly Schedule

Sunday	Monday	Tuesday	Wednesday	Thursday	Friday	Saturday
Practice Record:						

Lesson Assignments

Date: _____

Weekly Schedule

Sunday	Monday	Tuesday	Wednesday	Thursday	Friday	Saturday
Practice Record:						

Date: _____

Weekly Schedule

Sunday	Monday	Tuesday	Wednesday	Thursday	Friday	Saturday
Practice Record:						

Lesson Assignments

Date: _____

Weekly Schedule

Sunday	Monday	Tuesday	Wednesday	Thursday	Friday	Saturday
Practice Record:						

Date: _____

Weekly Schedule

Sunday	Monday	Tuesday	Wednesday	Thursday	Friday	Saturday
Practice Record:						

My Music Journal

Favorite Piano Pieces

_____

_____

_____

_____

_____

_____

_____

_____

_____

_____

_____

Favorite Piano Pieces

My Music Journal

Pieces I've Memorized

_____

_____

_____

_____

_____

_____

_____

_____

_____

_____

_____

My Music Journal

My Performances & Recitals

_____

_____

_____

_____

_____

My Music Books

_____

_____

_____

_____

_____

My Music Journal

Music I've Listened To

_____

_____

_____

_____

_____

Concerts I've Attended

_____

_____

_____

_____

_____

My Music Journal

Picture Album

My Music Journal

Picture Album

400 AD	600	800	1000	1200	1400

MUSIC

During the Middle Ages (also called the *Medieval Period*), the Roman Catholic church was the most powerful influence in European life. The church's music was a collection of ancient melodies called *plainsong* or *chant*, sung in unison (single line) with Latin words. The chants were organized in about 600 AD by Pope Gregory, and these official versions are known as *Gregorian chant*. Later, simple harmonies were added, and eventually the harmony parts became independent melodies sung with the main tune. This is called *polyphony*. Church music was written down using *neumes*, or square notes.

Outside the churches, traveling entertainers called *troubadours* or *minstrels* would sing songs about life and love in the language of the common people. This music was more lively and would often be accompanied by a drum, a wooden flute or an early form of the guitar called a *lute*.

- Plainsong
- Gregorian Chant
- Harmony
- Polyphony
- Troubadours

400 AD	600	800	1000	1200	1400

ART & LITERATURE

- Romanesque architecture
- Gothic architecture
- Dante, author (*The Divine Comedy*)
- Chaucer, author (*Canterbury Tales*)
- Donatello, artist (*David*)

400 AD	600	800	1000	1200	1400

WORLD EVENTS

- Fall of Roman Empire (*476 AD*)
- Charlemagne, Holy Roman Emperor
- First Crusade begins (*1096*)
- The Black Death (*bubonic plague*)
- Rise of European universities
- Muhammad, prophet of Islam faith
- The Magna Carta (*1215*)
- Hindu-Arabic numbers developed
- Gunpowder, compass, paper invented (*China*)
- Genghis Kahn rules Asia
- Marco Polo travels to China
- Mayan civilization
- Incan and Aztec civilizations

1450	1500	1550	1600

MUSIC

The era from about 1450–1600 was called the *Renaissance* ("rebirth") because people wanted to recreate the artistic and scientific glories of ancient Greece and Rome. It was also a time of discovery. The new printing press brought music to the homes of the growing middle class. European society became more *secular*, or non-religious, and concerts were featured in the halls of the nobility. An entertaining form of secular songs was the *madrigal*, sung by 4 or 5 voices at many special occasions. Instrumental music became popular, as new string, brass and woodwind instruments were developed.

A form of church music was the *motet*, with 3 or 4 independent vocal parts. In the new Protestant churches, the entire congregation sang *chorales*: simple melodies in even rhythms like the hymns we hear today. Important Renaissance composers were Josquin des Pres, Palestrina, Gabrielli, Monteverdi, William Byrd and Thomas Tallis.

• Protestant church music

• First printed music   • Madrigals

1450	1500	1550	1600

ART & LITERATURE

• Leonardo da Vinci, scientist/artist
(*Mona Lisa, The Last Supper*)

• Shakespeare, author
(*Romeo and Juliet, Hamlet*)

• Michelangelo, artist
(*Sistine Chapel, David*)

• Machiavelli,
author (*The Prince*)

1450	1500	1550	1600

WORLD EVENTS

• Gutenberg invents printing press *(1454)*   • Martin Luther ignites Protestant Reformation *(1517)*

• Columbus travels to America *(1492)*

• Magellan circles globe *(1519)*

• Copernicus begins modern astronomy *(1543)*

• First European contact with Japan *(1549)*

1600	1650	1700	1750

MUSIC

Music and the arts (and even clothing) became fancier and more dramatic in the *Baroque* era (about 1600–1750). Like the fancy decorations of Baroque church architecture, melodies were often played with *grace notes*, or quick nearby tones added to decorate them. Rhythms became more complex with time signatures, bar lines and faster-moving melodic lines. Our now familiar major and minor scales formed the basis for harmony, and chords were standardized to what we often hear today.

The harpsichord became the most popular keyboard instrument, with players often *improvising* (making up) their parts using the composer's chords and bass line. Violin making reached new heights in Italy. Operas, ballets and small orchestras were beginning to take shape, as composers specified the exact instruments, tempos and dynamics to be performed.

• Jean Baptiste Lully, French *(1632-1687)*

• Henry Purcell, English *(1658–1695)*

• Francois Couperin, French *(1668-1733)*

• Georg Philipp Telemann, German *(1681-1767)*

• Jean-Philippe Rameau, French *(1683-1764)*

• George Frideric Handel, German *(1685–1759)*

• Domenico Scarlatti, Italian *(1685–1757)*

J.S. Bach

1600	1650	1700	1750

ART & LITERATURE

• Cervantes, author *(Don Quixote)*

• Milton, author *(Paradise Lost)*

• Defoe, author *(Robinson Crusoe)*

• Rubens, artist *(Descent from the Cross)*

• Kabuki theater in Japan

• Rembrandt, artist *(The Night Watch)*

• Swift, author *(Gulliver's Travels)*

• Taj Mahal built *(1634–1653)*

1600	1650	1700	1750

WORLD EVENTS

• Salem witchcraft trials *(1692)*

• Galileo identifies gravity *(1602)*

• Louis XIV builds Versailles Palace *(1661–1708)*

• First English colony in America *(Jamestown, 1607)*

• Quebec founded by Champlain *(1608)*

• First slaves to America *(1619)*

• Isaac Newton *(1642-1727)* formulates principals of physics and math

THE CLASSICAL ERA

1750	1775	1800	1820

MUSIC

The *Classical* era, from about 1750 to the early 1800's, was a time of great contrasts. While patriots fought for the rights of the common people in the American and French revolutions, composers were employed to entertain wealthy nobles and aristocrats. Music became simpler and more elegant, with melodies often flowing over accompaniment patterns in regular 4-bar phrases. Like the architecture of ancient *Classical* Greece, music was fit together in "building blocks" by balancing one phrase against another, or one entire section against another.

The piano replaced the harpsichord and became the most popular instrument for the *concerto* (solo) with orchestra accompaniment. The string quartet became the favorite form of *chamber* (small group) music, and orchestra concerts featured *symphonies* (longer compositions with 4 contrasting parts or *movements*). Toward the end of this era, Beethoven's changing musical style led the way toward the more emotional and personal expression of Romantic music.

Haydn

Beethoven

Mozart

- Franz Haydn, Austrian (German) *(1732–1809)*
- Johann Christian Bach, German *(1735–1782)*
- Muzio Clementi, Italian *(1752–1832)*
- Wolfgang Amadeus Mozart, German *(1756–1791)*

- Ludwig van Beethoven, German *(1770-1827)*
- Antonio Diabelli, Italian *(1781-1858)*
- Friedrich Kuhlau, German *(1786-1832)*

1750	1775	1800	1820

ART & LITERATURE

- Samuel Johnson, author *(Dictionary)*

- Voltaire, author *(Candide)*

- Gainsborough, artist *(The Blue Boy)*

- *Encyclopedia Britannica*, first edition

- Wm. Wordsworth, author *(Lyrical Ballads)*

- Goethe, author *(Faust)*

- Goya, artist *(Witch's Sabbath)*

- Jane Austen, author *(Pride and Prejudice)*

1750	1775	1800	1820

WORLD EVENTS

- Ben Franklin discovers electricity *(1751)*

- American Revolution *(1775–1783)*

- French Revolution *(1789–1794)*

- Napoleon crowned Emperor of France *(1804)*

- Lewis and Clark explore northwest *(1804)*

- Metronome invented *(1815)*

- First steamship crosses Atlantic *(1819)*

1820   1840   1860   1880   1900

MUSIC

The last compositions of Beethoven were among the first of the new *Romantic* era, lasting from the early 1800's to about 1900. No longer employed by churches or nobles, composers became free from Classical restraints and expressed their personal emotions through their music. Instead of simple titles like *Concerto* or *Symphony*, they would often add descriptive titles like *Witches' Dance* or *To The New World*. Orchestras became larger, including nearly all the standard instruments we now use. Composers began to write much more difficult and complex music, featuring more "colorful" instrument combinations and harmonies.

Nationalism was an important trend in this era. Composers used folk music and folk legends (especially in Russia, eastern Europe and Scandinavia) to identify their music with their native lands. Today's concert audiences still generally prefer the drama of Romantic music to any other kind.

Schumann

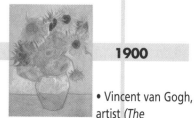

Brahms

- Franz Schubert, German *(1797-1828)*
- Felix Mendelssohn, German *(1809-1847)*
- Friedrich Burgmuller, German *(1806-1874)*
- Frederic Francois Chopin, Polish *(1810-1849)*
- Robert Schumann, German *(1810-1856)*
- Franz Liszt, Hungarian *(1811-1886)*
- Stephen Heller, German *(1813-1888)*
- Fritz Spindler, German *(1817-1905)*

- Cornelius Gurlitt, German *(1820-1901)*
- Cesar Auguste Franck, French *(1822-1890)*
- Johannes Brahms, German *(1833-1897)*
- Camille Saint-Saens, French *(1835-1921)*
- Modest Mussorgsky, Russian *(1839-1881)*
- Peter Ilyich Tchaikovsky, Russian *(1840-1893)*
- Edvard Grieg, Norwegian *(1844-1908)*

1820   1840   1860   1880   1900

ART & LITERATURE

- Charles Dickens, author *(The Pickwick Papers, David Copperfield)*
- Lewis Carroll, author *(Alice In Wonderland)*
- Vincent van Gogh, artist *(The Sunflowers)*
- Louisa May Alcott, author *(Little Women)*
- Rudyard Kipling, author *(Jungle Book)*
- Pierre Renoir, artist *(Luncheon of the Boating Party)*
- Jules Verne, author *(20,000 Leagues Under The Sea)*
- Harriet Beecher Stowe, author *(Uncle Tom's Cabin)*
- Claude Monet, artist *(Gare Saint-Lazare)*
- Mark Twain, author *(Tom Sawyer, Huckleberry Finn)*

1820   1840   1860   1880   1900

WORLD EVENTS

- First railroad *(1830)*
- American Civil War *(1861–1865)*
- Samuel Morse invents telegraph *(1837)*
- First photography *(1838)*
- Alexander Graham Bell invents telephone *(1876)*

- Edison invents phonograph, practical light bulb, movie projector *(1877–1888)*

| 1900 | 1925 | 1950 | 1975 | 2000 |

- Edward MacDowell, American *(1861–1908)*
- Claude Debussy, French *(1862–1918)*
- Alexander Scriabin, Russian *(1872-1915)*
- Sergei Rachmaninoff, Russian *(1873-1943)*
- Arnold Schoenberg, German *(1874-1950)*
- Maurice Ravel, French *(1875–1937)*
- Bela Bartok, Hungarian *(1881-1945)*
- Heitor Villa-Lobos, Brazilian *(1881-1959)*
- Igor Stravinsky, Russian *(1882–1971)*
- Sergei Prokofieff, Russian *(1891–1952)*
- Paul Hindemith, German *(1895-1963)*
- George Gershwin, American *(1898–1937)*
- Aaron Copland, American *(1900–1990)*
- Aram Khachaturian, Russian *(1903-1978)*
- Dmitri Kabalevsky, Russian *(1904-1986)*
- Dmitri Shostakovich, Russian *(1906-1975)*
- Samuel Barber, American *(1910-1981)*
- Norman Dello Joio, American *(1913-   )*
- Vincent Persichetti, American *(1915-   )*

MUSIC

The *20th century* was a diverse era of new ideas that "broke the rules" of traditional music. Styles of music moved in many different directions.

Impressionist composers Debussy and Ravel wrote music that seems more vague and blurred than the Romantics. New slightly-dissonant chords were used, and like Impressionist paintings, much of their music describes an impression of nature.

Composer Arnold Schoenberg devised a way to throw away all the old ideas of harmony by creating *12-tone* music. All 12 tones of the chromatic scale were used equally, with no single pitch forming a "key center."

Some of the music of Stravinsky and others was written in a *Neo-Classical* style (or "new" classical). This was a return to the Classical principals of balance and form, and to music that did *not* describe any scene or emotion.

Composers have experimented with many ideas: some music is based on the laws of chance, some is drawn on graph paper, some lets the performers decide when or what to play, and some is combined with electronic or other sounds.

Popular music like jazz, country, folk, and rock & roll has had a significant impact on 20th century life and has influenced great composers like Aaron Copland and Leonard Bernstein. And the new technology of computers and electronic instruments has had a major effect on the ways music is composed, performed and recorded.

| 1900 | 1925 | 1950 | 1975 | 2000 |

ART & LITERATURE

- Robert Frost, author *(Stopping by Woods on a Snowy Evening)*
- Pablo Picasso, artist *(Three Musicians)*
- J.R.R. Tolkien, author *(The Lord of the Rings)*
- F. Scott Fitzgerald, author *(The Great Gatsby)*
- Andy Warhol, artist *(Pop art)*
- Salvador Dali, artist *(Soft Watches)*
- Norman Mailer, author *(The Executioner's Song)*
- John Steinbeck, author *(The Grapes of Wrath)*
- Ernest Hemingway, author *(For Whom the Bell Tolls)*
- Andrew Wyeth, artist *(Christina's World)*
- George Orwell, author *(1984)*

| 1900 | 1925 | 1950 | 1975 | 2000 |

WORLD EVENTS

- First airplane flight *(1903)*
- Television invented *(1927)*
- Berlin Wall built *(1961)*
- Destruction of Berlin Wall *(1989)*
- World War I *(1914–1918)*
- World War II *(1939–1945)*
- John F. Kennedy assassinated *(1963)*
- First radio program *(1920)*
- Civil rights march in Alabama *(1965)*
- First satellite launched *(1957)*
- Man walks on the moon *(1969)*
- Vietnam War ends *(1975)*
- Personal computers *(1975)*

Notes:

48